There's A GOLDFISH In My Shoe!

By Valerie Sherrard

Illustrated by David Jardine

Tuckamore Books
a Creative Publishers Imprint

St. John's, Newfoundland and Labrador
2009

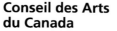  

We gratefully acknowledge the financial support of the Canada Council for the Arts,
the Government of Canada through the Book Publishing Industry Development Program (BPIDP),
and the Government of Newfoundland and Labrador through the Department of Tourism, Culture and
Recreation for our publishing program.

Illustrations and book design © 2009, David Jardine

Printed on acid-free paper

Published by
TUCKAMORE BOOKS
an imprint of CREATIVE BOOK PUBLISHING
a Transcontinental Inc. associated company
P.O. Box 8660, Station A
St. John's, Newfoundland and Labrador A1B 3T7

Printed in Canada by:
Transcontinental Inc.

Library and Archives Canada Cataloguing in Publication

Sherrard, Valerie
    There's a goldfish in my shoe! / Valerie Sherrard ; illustrated
by David Jardine.

Interest age level: For ages 5-10.
ISBN 978-1-897174-47-0

    I. Jardine, David II. Title.

PS8587.H3867T45 2009   jC813'.6   C2009-904669-5

My name is Oscar Ollie Brown;
I live in quite a pleasant town.
And my house looks a lot like yours,
With walls and windows, halls and doors.

But one thing is not normal here;
There's something wrong, I sadly fear.
For judging by what I have seen,
I think my mom is off her bean!

The things Mom says can be bizarre.
Like one day we were in the car,
And I was talking endlessly,
Until she turned and said to me:

"You talk *so* much for one so young!
Now, Oscar, can't you hold your tongue?"
This seemed quite odd, but Mom knows best,
And so I followed her request.

A tongue is rather hard to hold,
But boys like me do what we're told.
I used both hands and grabbed on tight,
And held my tongue with all my might!

Then as I waited to be praised,
My mother said, as though amazed,
"Now what on earth is this about?
Don't put your fingers in your mouth!"

You might think she'd make up her mind!
Not *my* mom – she's the changing kind!

My goldfish Slick (a fine fish name)
Is short and round and pretty tame.
I hold his bowl and watch him play,
But then it came, that awful day!

While Slick was swimming happily,
His big eyes staring out at me,
('Cause that's the way a fish has fun),
My mother hollered, "Oscar! Son!"

"Drop everything and come here quick."
And so I dropped the bowl and Slick!
It landed with a bounce or two,
And left Slick splashing – in my shoe!

I rushed right to my mother's side,
Like I'd been told, but then she cried:
"Land sakes alive! Look what you've done!
Go save that fish! Be quick now, run!"

I raced back in to rescue Slick.
His eyes were crossed – he looked quite sick!
His fins were flapping weak and slow;
His cheeks had lost their golden glow.

A shoe was not the place for him;
There wasn't even room to swim.
I fetched a jug of water quick,
Filled up his bowl and plopped in Slick.

Poor Slick had suffered quite a shock,
Because of Mom's peculiar talk!

So *many* things Mom says are odd.
Like once when my Great Auntie Maude
Was bringing us some homemade jam,
My mother told me, "Be a lamb."

I thought I'd heard her wrong that time,
Until the doorbell rang its chime.
And Mom repeated, "Auntie's here!
Be *sure* to be a lamb, my dear."

I'd never been a lamb before,
But I got right down on the floor,
And bleated "*BAA!*" with all my might.
Then Auntie dropped her jam in fright.

My mother soothed their nerves with tea,
And guess who cleaned the jam! Yes, me!
That sticky mess, that gooey red,
Which never will be spread on bread.

I heard Mom say, "I cannot guess
Why Oscar caused this awful mess!"
Then Auntie tapped her head and smiled,
And called me a peculiar child.

The strange things Mother asks of me,
Just seem to go on endlessly!

One day she told me, "Keep an eye
On Mister Tom. That cat will try
To swipe our fish, this lovely cod.
And we don't want food Tom has pawed!"

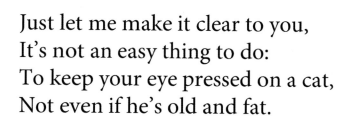

Just let me make it clear to you,
It's not an easy thing to do:
To keep your eye pressed on a cat,
Not even if he's old and fat.

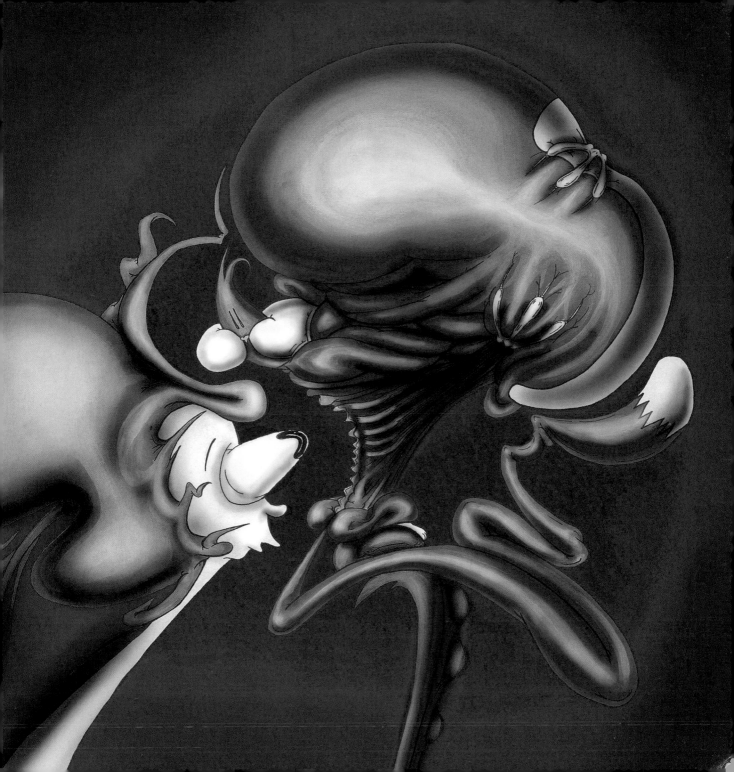

All through the house that naughty cat
Raced madly while he hissed and spat.
He swiped at me and ran to crouch
Beyond my reach behind the couch.

When Mom returned, I thought she'd frown,
And call me, "Oscar Ollie Brown."
And scold me for the wrong I'd done,
But *this* time she said, "Great job, Son!"

What would *you* think? What would you *do*
If *your* mom said strange things to *you*?

"Drop everything, come on the run,
Now be a lamb, or hold your tongue!"
I'll do them, be they daft or no,
Because my mother tells me so.